LEGO® friends

A Puppy Tale

By Sierra Harimann

Illustrated by Pixel Mouse House LLC

SCHOLASTIC INC.

ISBN 978-0-545-51754-6

12 11 10 9 8 7 6 5 4 3 2 1 MIX
Paper from
responsible sources
FSC FSC® C020056   13 14 15 16 17 18/0

Printed in the U.S.A.   40
First printing, August 2013

It was a beautiful day in Heartlake City. Mia was taking her puppy, Charlie, to the vet.

Andrea was leaving the City Park Café when she spotted Mia.

Hi, Mia! Are you taking Charlie to the vet?

He doesn't look very happy. Wait, I know! Stay right here!

AROOOO!

Andrea went into the café and came back with some homemade dog biscuits.

If you're a good boy at the vet, Charlie, you can have some treats!

Woof! Woof!

Soon, the girls reached the Heartlake City Vet. Olivia was there giving animals checkups.

Olivia began Charlie's exam.

His heart sounds strong!

BA-BUMP! BA-BUMP!

Let's see how much you weigh. You gained half a pound!

Arf!

Mia chased Charlie down the street . . .

Charlie, *come back!*

The girls drove all over Heartlake City. But they couldn't spot Charlie anywhere.

Just then . . .

Wait, look over there. Charlie's collar!

The crumbs led the girls to Ambersands Beach.

It's so crowded. We'll never find him.

Look! There're Emma and Jacob. Maybe they saw Charlie.

Soon, Jacob and Stephanie were soaring high above Ambersands Beach.

23

The plane flew closer to the beach.

Come in, Olivia. We spotted some paw prints near the shoreline.

Copy that, Jacob.

Jacob and Stephanie spotted the friends below.

They found Charlie!

Yeah!

Stephanie helped Jacob land the plane.

31

The girls spent the rest of the afternoon at the beach.

Hey Charlie, want to play fetch?

I think he's saying, "yes."

Just promise you'll come *right back*!

Arooooo!